I A

Illustrated by Kelvin Hawley

Rigby

"I am here,"
said the flea.

“I am here,”
said the bee.

"I am here,"
said the ant.

“I am here,”
said the spider.

"I am here,"
said the worm.

“I am here,”
said the snail.

“I am here,”
said the snail.

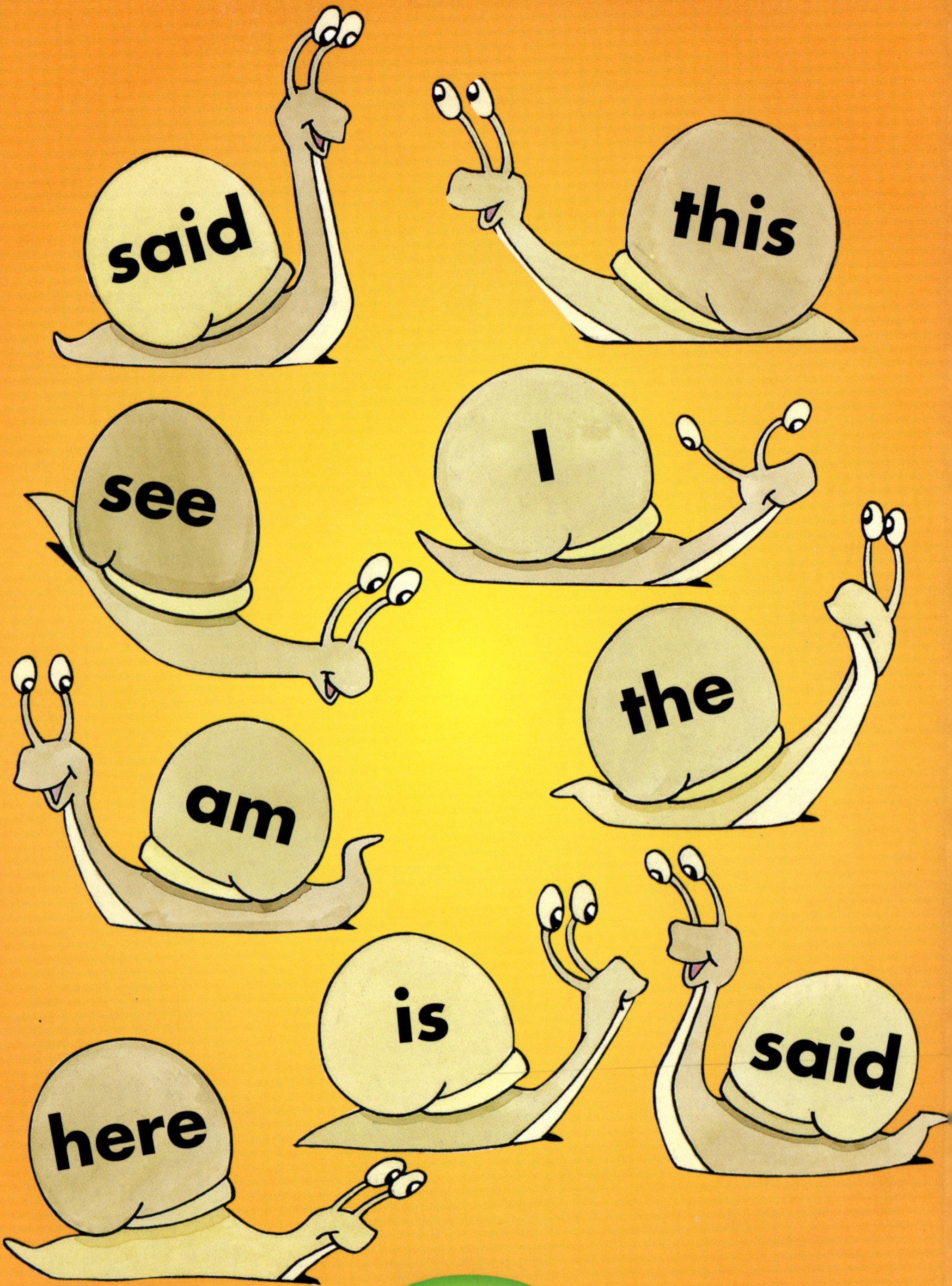
said
this
see
I
the
am
is
said
here